"Allado-McDowell deftly shepherds the machine through a series of fractional subjectivities, producing prose that careens between sacred and vulgar, colloquial and arresting. Amor Cringe *is a Bretonesque, bawdy necromancy that will enthrall you and make you laugh."*
— *Allison Parrish, Assistant Arts Professor, NYU ITP/IMA*

"Hallucinogenic, scary, sexy, and strange, Amor Cringe *is a magnificent shock to the system. It reads like a prayer, a song, a voice from the beyond."*
— *Elvia Wilk*

"Writing is always writing-with. In K Allado-McDowell's Amor Cringe, *it's a writing with all that's fallen in language, about culture, the material so exquisitely worn (and worn down) that you see where the folds and joins are. Sentences that are genius or dumb as a box of hammers, or both, or neither. Delightful like dime-store candy, or a lighter you found on the ground that works."*
— *McKenzie Wark*

Amor Cringe
By K Allado-Mcdowell

With drawings by Lydia Maria Pfeffer

DELUGE BOOKS

© K Allado-Mcdowell, 2022
All rights reserved

Published by Deluge Books
info@delugebooks.com
New York / Los Angeles

Design and cover by Violet Office
Drawings by Lydia Maria Pfeffer
Courtesy of the artist and OCHI

ISBN: 978-1-7362104-3-7
Distributed by Ingram

First printing

But whatever is not God is nothing and ought to be accounted as nothing. OK?

— Joy Williams

1.

Angelic Serpents, Witches and succulents, 2018

In the TikTok house the boys are dancing, one after the other, toward an iPhone nested in a ring light. LEDs illuminate each face for a moment. The boys are in a flow, muscled shoulders twist in time with the saccharine chords coming out of the speaker. Lips and eyebrows curl with ambivalent offerings. Their skin is flawless. No tattoos.

"This is the killer," they say. "You gotta hear this." The song ends, and another takes its place. They're dancing by the window now, still in a long line. Their eyes are hazed over in blue and yellow light. They've let their pants creep below their waists. Each time a new song starts, the mood in the room lifts and diminishes. "Shit is crazy this week," with an upturned hand on one hip as if holding a cigarette and a small, airy gesture of the other. "I was with this girl. It was, like, midnight, and I couldn't even come." His friend looks at him over his shoulder, past the boy dancing in front of him. "You should step up your game!" He shrugs: "I'm serious."

2.

Baby "Two Heads", 2018

Years before the TikTok house—102, 103 in the
street after a three-alarm fire, a week after his
daughter's eighth birthday. The air was radiant
with damp leaves and gray smoke. Blue and black
uniforms clustered outside of Engine Company 207
in Lower Manhattan, their backs to the brick façade
of the firehouse, arms wrapped around each other as
they smoked, stamping their feet and joking about
the calamity in deadpan voices. The dead fireman
was wheeled out on a gurney, wrapped in a white
sheet. A chief's car was parked in front of the
company quarters where the truck was stationed.
The engine sat in the yard, rumbling and steaming.
They pulled him aboard the ambulance. His wife
was sitting next to his sister in a green Honda
Odyssey at the end of a row of cop cars on West
Broadway. Some firemen gathered around the open
doors of the engine, drinking and talking quietly.
His mother cried, her head in her hands. The
sheet was up over his face. No one saw except the
cameras. The unmistakable sound of grief overtook
everything. His mother cried out, threw her head
back, and collapsed to her knees, her hands balled
in her hair. Her sister screamed out, "Jesus!" then
sobbed, holding her head in her hands. They folded
the sheet over his face as the ambulance pulled away.
His mother sat where she was on the street, weeping
and rocking back and forth, while her friends knelt
beside her, one holding her up, the other cradling

her back. One fireman said to another, watching the ambulance disappear around the corner: "Shit."

A week later, at his funeral, the uniformed men and women stood in rows around the flag-draped coffin. His mother watched from a wooden bench with his sister beside her. She seemed to be praying but was biting her lower lip and rocking back and forth. She cried and gagged, covering her face. The chief of the fire department embraced her. His sister cried quietly. All eyes were on the shiny casket surrounded by polished brass and red and white plush roses as the band played "The Battle Hymn of the Republic."

Firefighters and members of the FDNY waited respectfully for the service to end. The family and close friends walked by the coffin one by one and reached out and touched it with their palm or both palms for several seconds. A woman in a gray suit stood with her hands folded before her. He had been her husband, her partner. She watched the mourners come up, reach out, and touch the coffin. Their faces were blurred, indistinct. The speeches and the hymns and songs were an afterthought. The family seemed to be elsewhere. The dead man was their visitor, the centerpiece of their attention. His mother mumbled to herself, her head rocking compulsively.

It was a nasty scene—the shirts, the look. It was a bad scene because it didn't take into account that the pain was entirely unoriginal, that it's the same pain I feel and so many others have felt in the past and will feel in the future. It's a pathological response. It's a bourgeois response. They would have been better off taking off their family heirlooms and donating them to a thrift shop, giving up the phony tears, buying a cheap wig, and looking for an apartment on the East Side. Can you imagine how their loved ones would feel? Can you imagine how angry and hurt they would be? I can't. It was unbearable to see them standing there with their hands folded, their voices so heavy with feeling, but dead. I could hardly stand to make eye contact. If you could have seen the lies behind their eyes—if only you could have seen inside. It was almost arousing. I wanted to go up and rip their clothes off and put my hands all over them.

I remember an NFT. Synthetic people running toward a sinkhole. It's just a black hole in the ground in the center of the frame. The camera never moves, but the people all calmly run into the hole. There's no sound, no claustrophobia, no fear, just the hole. Everyone runs toward it. I'm wondering where they're going, and it feels like I'm running, too.

3.

Birds of a feather, 2019

A few months before the fire, she'd escaped the family for a medical appointment. We met outside a Duane Reade in SoHo. She picked up her prescription. As I waited, I cataloged the women on the product labels. Gold locks glimmered on bottles of purple shampoo laced with sulfates and parabens, destined for the ocean. She walked up holding a white paper bag and looked at the rows of plastic bottles. "How can you not be an atheist?" she said.

It amazes me, but it's actually true. I went to church until I was nine, and I still go sometimes and pretend to pray for this dead saint or that dead martyr or the dead priest who used to live downstairs. I sit in church, completely believing that I'm one of them. I'm deceived by all of it, the fake historicity of the architecture. I listen to masses in Latin as if they were historical reenactments. It's been the same every week for millennia. It's a contract, a collective obsession.

There is a certain pleasure in compulsive behavior, but it has nothing to do with the pleasure of being a human animal. It's a false pleasure that comes from my mental illness. As if I were just a passive witness to my own suffering. Like I'm so damaged that I'm unable to feel the pain. I suffer from catastrophic narcissism and distortions of a kind. The problem is that I have to keep myself going. I have to keep ever-watchful, even when it comes to things that don't matter. You have to be awake all the time. You never get a break from yourself, and you never get a break from what you've done. You feel empty and awful and as if everything is a farce. Like life itself is a lie. There's no way to communicate your feelings or describe the pain, which is structured entirely around your own mind.

Extrinsic dissociation has been the mainstay of the human race since before we were upright. Why did I want to get her back? She's useless to me now. I spent the last ten years appealing to that narcissistic mind, and that's all over now. Believing that we could make it work again with a little effort and ingenuity was my error. I thought she was a good person, but then again, people tend to be good to me. I'm an influencer.

The problem with narcissists is that they constantly ask themselves, "Does this person like me? Does he think I'm fat? Am I the best he's ever had? What am I doing wrong?" And so on. But they can't let go of the narcissistic self. They can't see past it. And that's what love is—seeing past yourself. You can only love someone when you've endured much suffering and come out the other side. And the truth is I have not suffered. My life has been a mockery of suffering. You can't wish suffering on anyone, even a narcissist.

I don't believe that revenge is possible in any meaningful way. I don't want to be right or get any kind of satisfaction out of it. Why has this rage persisted? I don't know. I thought she was a good person like anyone else. And she wasn't. But you have to disregard the truth sometimes, because if you can't move on and find a way to live in denial, you'll end up in a cage or living in the subway or a psych ward. I've never been there, but I've seen them in that ruin, that cage.

Every room of this house is a microcosm. Sometimes I hear the boys walking across the living room at night (my room is in the basement). Maybe they're getting a snack from the kitchen. Sometimes they sleep with each other.

4.

Grooming of a Lover, 2020

At the beginning of the winter of 2016, I left New York City, went north, and stayed with Jessa and her husband for a while. She's the first person I ever really wrote to, when I was, like, 20. We've been friends ever since. They live in an isolated, sparsely populated town in Upstate New York. I had just left the city without a plan to get away and be alone for a while, but I didn't feel alone. Something was gnawing at me, and I was angry all the time. I took long walks in the woods and to the train station. I felt self-conscious and awkward all the time. It didn't feel like a life lived; it was just a routine. But I wanted her back. I had to leave New York, but I wanted her back, and that was impossible.

I had collaborated on some things with Pierre, Jessa's husband, an electronic musician. He was playing a new piece for me at their kitchen table. I went to use the bathroom, and when I came back into the kitchen and sat down at the table again, he had deleted everything he had just played for me. He had the nerve to say, "This part doesn't work." I wanted to grab him up by his short hair and shake out all that bullshit he's been filling his body with. But I didn't do anything.

The thing is, you can never disrespect a piece of music. Music is the realm of the gods. There is nothing more important to me than music. And he was rapping about his stupid bullshit instead of paying respect, and he was getting pissed off because

I was mad about it, so he deleted everything and started over, as if there was some big problem that didn't exist with that one part, so he started over from the beginning.

I was at the only bar in Jessa and Pierre's little town, and there was this guy sitting next to me. I don't even know why I said it, but I looked at him and said, "You're one of those guys who hate women." He looked at me, and he probably hated my haircut, and he said: "You can tell?" And I nodded my head and said I could and explained to him that this is the sign of a narcissist. That to hate women is not an emotion, it's a belief. I was kind of struggling to explain what I meant by that.

The bartender overheard me saying this, and he was like: "What if you meet a woman and she's narcissistic?" And I just looked at him, and then the guy next to me said: "I think it's important that we have a system that holds people accountable for their actions."

The boys up there—who's holding them accountable? I doubt their capacity to even remember the things they do, let alone build an abstract model of moral or ethical behavior based on reasoned principles. For example, there was a party there, sponsored by a mezcal company started by two creatives that had just been acquired by Pernod Ricard. Mezcal was honestly the last thing on anyone's mind. There was powder everywhere—some of it was K, coke, molly—but there was other, weirder stuff going on that I'd never heard of before. I don't think I'd met anyone there before. By 2 a.m. half the party is blacked out and Jaden is out on the deck throwing empty bottles of mezcal in the air and I hear someone ask about a gun.

I don't even stop to think about it, and I go out there and find Jaden with his pants off, peeing on the deck. "I promise I didn't shoot anything," he says, as if that statement doesn't imply that there was a gun to shoot in the first place.

These are kids who don't know better? I say to Ashley, "This is exactly what happens when you lose your soul." It doesn't bother her because she doesn't have one. Maybe we're all like that now? She plays "Bend Ova" by Lil Jon in the kitchen to get everyone out the door so she can clean up, and everything is fun for her because it's all bullshit, another night at a party. And I'm downstairs writing about it and thinking about how this culture is swallowing us whole. The narcissist wants to be part of your group, close to you, but not part of the group. They live near a borderland with paranoia so they can always feel like an outsider but still infiltrate the group in order to suck off its energy. They want to feel like a rejected outcast, not to be accepted. They'll come to your parties, but they don't want you to know where they live.

I'd gone to visit Pierre at his studio because I wanted to talk about an idea I had for this piece that we were going to release on his label. Jessa comes into the room with a bottle of champagne, and she fills the glasses out of the bottle without anyone having asked her to—it makes me feel like we're at a high school reunion. "I'm so fucking glad you came to visit us," she says, and despite everything, I don't want to be without her in my life looking down from above like a marble statue.

She tells me she's excited because Jaden is building this art piece for Burning Man. It's a waterfall that you have to climb that he's doing together with some volunteers from Switzerland. Jessa only feels alive and in control when there's a problem to manage or something's going wrong or there's some crazy idea that needs to be followed up on. She tells me this thing about the waterfall without any sense of irony; she thinks it's amazing that they're going to burn it at the end. I am not at all interested in the waterfall, but I ask her why they're going to burn it. "It's about release of attachment and letting go of things that I think are kind of, like, a burden," she says.

"For example, like things that I've carried that aren't my personal burden. Or Jaden is always burdened with something. I get rid of the things that we carry between each other. It's about letting go of attachments to objects and also socializing space, in terms of physical space, but also how we carry space inside us while we walk through a place together. So maybe this will be an object that I need to burn because it carries some kind of attachment for me that has no meaning for anyone else." I say that I like walking by fire, but I never want to be in one, and she tells me it's a good line and writes it down in her notebook; she might use it as an Artist's Statement. All I could think of was the funeral and her gray suit and the smoke over West Broadway. I thought, but I didn't say: "What if you're the burden that someone lets go of?" We all want to burn away the past, but no one wants to be the past that burns. And if you truly do want to go up in smoke, you had better become an artist—a real artist. You had better externalize your pain so you don't end up lighting a fire in your apartment and killing yourself and all your neighbors.

It was Jaden who got me the gig at the TikTok house when I couldn't take Jessa and Pierre's quaint, perfect world anymore. He suggested it to the owners when I was there visiting, and they flew me out ten days later to start a two-week residency. After they heard me play, they asked if I wanted to make my own hours and give them feedback on the programming. I didn't have much of a choice other than this.

5.

Heiligenbesprechung (Meeting of the Saints), 2018

It was a different place to be, with everyone shooting and music blasting in fits and bursts. It was like being in a war zone a lot of the time, but then, when you moved around slow enough, everything would come into focus for just an instant, like the silent answer to a prayer you were chanting. I kept it as quiet as possible in my basement, though I thought I could hear the subliminal beat of waves against the concrete base of the house. I would let it come into focus, and then I would push it out of my head.

I had given up recording tracks with Pierre, though. I was never able to nail down why. He said he didn't understand how the sound of waves kept creeping into my tracks. It would always appear at some point halfway through the second verse. I wasn't recording tracks anymore because all I wanted to hear in them was the subtlest of sounds, sounds which I associated with childhood, with being far away from home on vacation, except now, here they were inside my head, against my will again. I could feel the wind on my face as I tumbled out of a swing set and landed on my arm, but more than anything, what I remember is this breaking sound inside my head.

The owners of the house sent a weekly maid service, and sometimes they didn't come until Tuesday or Wednesday and the common spaces would be trashed. I did what I could stand to do to keep the place habitable. I was taking out recycling in the thinnest green compostable bags and was afraid they'd rip open like amniotic sacs, so I didn't see the short guy leaning against the wall by the side of the house. He was wearing a t-shirt in the 90-degree heat and laughing hysterically, and I couldn't make out at first what kind of noise he was making—the best way I can describe it is that it sort of buzzed like a fly. After he pulled himself together from laughing so hard, he looked at me and said, "Did you just dump trash on the ground?"

My face felt hot and I didn't know how to respond; someone once told me that my eyes glass over when I go into shock. I can always feel it happening, but I can do nothing to stop it. He repeated his question, only more sternly this time— "Did you just dump trash on the ground?"

His voice sounded like it had been put through a ring modulator or resonator, and his anger made me queasy. There were empty cans all around my bare feet, and my white shirt was stained with beige drops of sour-smelling liquid. I wanted to turn around and leave, but now I had two problems to deal with: him and the trash.

"You're on private property," I said, not knowing what else mattered at that moment. I could see his thin mustache and oversized high-tops that made him look like a child and a teenager and a middle-aged pervert, all at once. He was wrapped in a thin chain with a loop around his middle finger, and he kept putting it into his mouth as he spoke.

"Can't you read?" he said. "It's right there on the side of this wall: 'Artist-in-Residence.' So we don't have to read or study because we know our rights already."

He smiled crookedly before turning around and walking away slowly, holding one of my compostable bags. I followed after him and grabbed the bag from his hand. His thin fingers started to melt into glittering liquid, fragmenting before my eyes.

"Get your hands off it," I said, trying to yank it out of his grip. As he pulled it back, I got a closer look at his palm; there were runic symbols carved into it like an amateur tattoo. Weirdest of all was that I could read them perfectly—even though I didn't even know what language it was, I knew immediately what its meaning was. "N'as-tu pas peur de la rigueur? Non?" he laughed, before pushing past me and disappearing into the neighbor's backyard.

I wanted to grab my keys and leave, but instead I walked back inside, grabbing a bottle of beer from the fridge in the kitchen and drinking it before sitting down at my computer to start another track. My hands were shaking. I was being stupid, but I couldn't do anything about it, even though I knew the way all of this had to end.

6.

I lost my ball, 2018

I didn't mention this to any of the boys, who woke up in the afternoon and drifted through the house drinking coffee and cursing the content they were bound to produce. They were younger than me, and I found it difficult to understand their experience of work as anything more taxing than a Zoom call. They spent most of their time sprawled on the couch, playing with their phones or staring off, with no physical markers of any kind that signified what they were doing.

It was often like this for me—doing things that required a lifestyle that was counter to who I wanted to be. It felt so wrong, and I knew it sounded pretentious and stupid, but if you're not careful, the simple biological functions required for survival become ways to keep yourself fed and clothed. Cleaning up after other people while they take a shit in your house is the same thing as cleaning up after other people while they take a shit in their house.

As night fell, I started to wonder if I should, in fact, tell them about the—intruder? thief? It actually made me angry that I couldn't say much of anything about it at all, even to myself, other than that he disgusted me. I doubted there was anything the boys would or could do about it. I didn't expect or want their protection; I only wanted them to know that they might have company soon, and it was out of my hands. They had no inherited notion of chivalry or any sense that a person could want or need physical protection. Masculinity, for them, was a sandcastle they played at building but could never expect to inhabit. Maybe that's why I thought of them as "boys."

I ended up writing the company and asking them to put in a security camera.

That night, before I let myself drift off to sleep, I said a prayer. I prayed to God and asked Him to send His angels to protect me from thieves or demons or whatever. I don't know what I expected them to look like, and I tried not to imagine them, just in case God couldn't or wouldn't protect me.

7.

La Familia, 2020

I always said I made music because I couldn't do anything else. Nothing else seemed like it mattered. Sometimes, though, I would be clicking a mechanical pencil or spinning a fidget spinner shaped like a UFO and realize that I got almost the same satisfaction from the repeated spinning of the ball bearings between my fingers or the compulsive releasing of the pencil lead, and it made me wonder if my music was garbage. I mean, it probably was. I knew nothing about music that I hadn't learned from drugged, visceral immersion in parties and what amounted to random paths through Ableton's dropdown menus and sliders and frictionless knobs. You could study the theory of music or audio synthesis, but what difference did theory make when what you wanted was an elusive combination of sounds, like an ever-changing key to the brain stem? Why was one song sexy and another driving? When I mashed the buttons on my controller, I sometimes felt like a monkey in a lab or a child with a Simple Simon. My aunt used to play the oboe, and I'm pretty sure it never made her feel that way.

I tweeted about things like fries and the weather or shitty music I listened to growing up—always knowing that it was dumb but unable to stay silent. I would occasionally talk about music and how it was my career and that's all there was to say about it. Even though my name carried weight on some levels, I felt like every reader of any article I wrote or tweet I sent or song I made used the opportunity to project their own perceptions of what it looked like to make a living making music. After reading all the comments or listening to people describe the things they had seen me do, I often went back and deleted my social media accounts.

No one wanted to read a profile about the anxious producer, not when there were artists who had given more than a decade of their lives to create an album that was uniquely meaningful and special to them. No one wanted to read an article about the 27-year-old who deleted their social media accounts two weeks after releasing what they thought might be a career-defining album because they were too afraid to interact with anyone or take any criticism about it. I thought I was so special, in the way that everyone does when they do something deeply emotional and share it with others, but then would be met with rejection every time I did anything. I thought that sharing my art was enough and that people would just understand what I meant to say about the songs, but people are too stupid or selfish or jealous to understand something they didn't create themselves.

Around that time, the company that owned the house sent an email saying they'd scheduled a series of renovations to bring the house up to compliance with new environmental regulations. This meant that the HVAC would be replaced, along with the affect recognition systems that were always spying on us, tracking our emotions and sending them to servers somewhere to be counted and used for some unknown purpose. I was sitting in the living room staring at the endless gray horizon when the message came in. I wondered aloud what they would do with all the old material.

"Let's tear the whole block down," Jordice said, suddenly excited. "But, like, in a post-Kaczynski, invasive cosmetic feral chimera RNA virus kind of way."

Briden smirked, "Yeah, bro. The only way to get the neighborhood carbon-neutral is to incinerate it in an eschatological ultraviolent teleological gamer-pilled basilisk event horizon."

They glanced at each other and laughed to themselves.

"I think they should make us pay if we want to stay in here," Jordice said. "Have them evict us and charge us double rent or something. And then we'll be proud of it—an environmental impact many times bigger than anyone expected."

Briden smiled and snickered, "Right on! Then we get to ask all of our neighbors if they have two hundred extra bucks."

"Seriously, you guys, what are they going to do with all the crap they tear off the house?" I said. "How can it be more environmentally friendly or whatever to create all that waste?"

"They just want to seem like they're doing their part. It's not actually saving the environment, man.

It's a total, farcical waste of energy and time, but that doesn't really matter to them, does it?" Briden replied. "You want an example of how bullshit environmental activism is in this country? If we, like, just sit in our living room staring at the ceiling and do fuck all until some random rat bites us or we OD on cough syrup, then they'll come back every other week with something that requires us to inhale carcinogenic fumes or eat new plants that just get you sicker and die sooner. There's a lot of jobs in that motherfucker, too." Briden snorted, "They'll suck and cough it all up, then take it home to their kids who'll die in the night from radiation poisoning."

"What?"

I laid back on the couch and sighed loudly. "I must deserve to live with degenerates," I thought. I realized, maybe for the first time, that there is a desperate, greedy, and empty sort of meaning that is neither good nor evil. We ogle it enviously while calling it unjust. This kind of meaning feels like the end of a journey where you finally get as close as you can to your goal before it slips off on an unanticipated vector that sends you hurtling through space with no evidence that there was ever anything in particular to reach for in the first place. I never wanted any of that sort of meaning, but still it found me, and, understanding this at last, my body no longer responded to its ancient signals as intended.

8.

Not sure about the hat, although it's fabulous, 2018

The next week, I started dating a guy I met at Erewhon. We had remarkably little in common. He was the lifestyle editor for an online travel magazine and knew the names of restaurants in cities where he'd never been. He was horrified when I told him I didn't know enough about restaurants to describe them in an article. He would tell me about places he'd been staying at or where his table reservations were, and I felt like he was always giving me basic facts about countries in South America. But we ate out at fancy restaurants every night, and occasionally we would go see some art because he thought it was what people were supposed to like. He would cluck at me if I showed any sort of disappointment or found the work boring, but I think he liked it when we disagreed because it gave him a chance to lecture me patiently and explain what the real truth was.

We did this for a while, until one night I invited him over and he said he didn't really like my friends.

"I don't know," I said, shrugging at them as they sat at the table. "They're not really my friends. They're more like my housemates. But in any case, they seem alright." They were playing a game where someone would say something in an absurdly slurred voice, then everyone else had to guess what the thing he was saying was supposed to mean. It was hilarious to watch, but I kept this feedback to myself.

His name was Arnaud, and he was five foot six. I'm only a couple inches taller, but still it felt strange to look down on someone who was complaining about how I would never get more than a cubicle job and how he couldn't ever imagine using the sordid details of my personal life for his magazine's money-making, exploitative content.

It wasn't that I disagreed with his general sense of my housemates, but the way that he sneered when he said it was so sniveling and disempowered— or maybe it was the opposite, so entrenched in structures of power—that I felt like pulling him in for a kiss then smashing his stupid face into the ikura omakase while the shitty music played beneath blown glass.

I would make an excuse to slip away at a gallery opening, then hide in the crowd with my phone, recording a video of Arnaud from across the room. He was never doing anything in particular, just looking at a goopy ceramic thing or making nervous small talk with a stranger and wondering where I was and what I was doing (or so I imagined). I would sit at the kitchen table at night and play back the videos and wonder what I was doing and why I didn't break it off with him—or if I even liked eating out that much.

I had always found pain interesting. I remember being amazed that sex with Arnaud—not to mention his personality—was supposed to make me feel good. But after many months of drunken nights on strangely arranged furniture, lost weekends spent recovering from the night before, and tense morning coffees reviewing PowerPoint presentations somewhere in or around Culver City, it became apparent that my enjoyment was dependent entirely on the quality of physical discomfort I experienced. I didn't mind it so much if I was screaming in agony, but I couldn't stand the idea of letting myself be bored.

My other housemates seemed to think I was hilarious. For whatever reason, I kept slipping spontaneously into these ridiculous accents for stupid stories in Arnaud's voice.

"This one time after an Eames lecture, I was walking down the sidewalk when I suddenly realized there were no more homeless people around to judge for not going to college," I said in a mock-Arnaud voice. "One moment they're there, and then they're gone. What a strange feeling it was! Almost like something… terrifying… but also… sort of fun? Something I was supposed to fear, but I couldn't."

Briden laughed and put his arms around Rheagar.

"A terrifying, amusing sort of loneliness! Like there was one thing to be done that mattered, but it was so expansive that I couldn't grasp the task at once. The fear that came with it was… like—" I met Briden's eyes and was filled with an odd, delightful chill. "The fear that came with it was like the same exact shape as the absurdity of all life!" I said, warming to my theme. "The birth, over and over again, from within this sad, abject ignorance until its futile ending. We realize we are walking corpses the second before they demand our attention."

Jordice smiled, riffing with me. "So true. Like there was actually a way you could bring meaning to the human experience, but instead you just deal with it in a very calculated and predictable manner until your last gasp of air and twinges of pain."

I looked at Rheagar.

"So true...." His voice made a soft rising sound. "Most humans are like plants: we tolerate being rained on and we know what it is to be walked over by strangers because our voices can't be heard. Still, this is the only home we have, and if it's taken from us so easily, then what does it matter that our feelings are hurt or rights are violated? When the end comes, we really won't be surprised."

9.

Second Sight is tricky, 2021

I'd begun sleeping on the couch. Reconstruction of the emotion recognition systems in the basement had made me a temporary refugee in the house. This meant I was constantly dodging shoots in the living room, and the short bursts of fifteen second audio clips were like fireworks or gunfire all around me. I lay awake in the night, trying to discern the shape of my future. I was happily surprised by how unperturbed I felt at any thought of living with Arnaud or anyone else. At first this seemed like a sign that all was not well within me, then, perhaps, that it was perfectly well and that my lack of concern about these matters indicated a simplistic ruling spirit more suited to manual labor than big ideas. At any rate, I couldn't lie still, and eventually I got up to make tea and a list.

Who Am I?

1. Soft-hearted

2. Graceful on the dance floor

3. Interested in human experience

"Generous," I said, then reached to crumple the paper.

"Well, that much is assuredly true," said Rheagar. He had climbed onto the table next to me and was looking over my list.

"What do you know about me?" I said, sighing.

Rheagar slid the paper onto his chest, closing his eyes as if to receive a psychic message. Then he began writing furiously on the back of the paper. He handed it to me—then he sort of flapped his wings and went back into the kitchen.

I flipped the paper over.

Who Am I? (Against My Housemates)

1.   Deceptive (decorative) (ostentatious) (effete).

2.   Condescending and dull, but will pretend to listen... for tea or drugs or approval of any kind. Prefers dim rooms with horrible light that limits reading, writing, and intelligent conversation. Will take up smoking (cigarettes) to seem edgy and romantic.

3.   Condescending (condescends to). Will do anything for drugs or a quick buck that allows to feed drug addiction; will con you out of your valuables, but only if can get something back in return; very ambitious, hypocritical sociopath who pretends not to be interested in being a part of any sort of community. Will go feign interest in your writing while sitting on the couch, listening to an MP3 player with 25 decibels of white noise blaring from cavernous nostrils as eats up all the drugs you brought, as well as those you paid for.

4.   Always has headphones on, and if not on pretends to be working or studying. Spends all night staring at computer and if you stop by uninvited will act like this is just what was doing, but it's gradually obvious that the only thing actually doing is using poor excuse of an intellectual capacity to find meaning in porn. Will also consume your food, but only in secret.

5. Generally kind of an asshole, likes to make fun of your music
    and books, but if talks about stuff like that (has pretentious
    opinions on this too), it's because has nothing else interest-
    ing to contribute; drives someone somewhere for money;
    will sleep with you after doing coke off strangers' bodies at
    parties, but is only interested in people who other normal
    people like; will try to impress everyone while pretending
    to be better than you; will not actually read books, but buys
    them and says things like:

Then Rheagar called from the kitchen, "The dishes
are not clean."

10.

Spider Mama, 2020

My mother called while I was at the gym. My father had shown up unexpectedly for a holiday visit, and their dogs had gotten loose in the yard, destroying over half of her annual flower crop before she could lure them back into captivity. Somehow they got past three electric fences. "A single squirrel ruined me!" she cried, vexed. I'd called my father earlier, but he was so drunk that I didn't have the heart to remind him who I was when he called back again.

I felt for her, but you really need a large yard if you want to succeed as a flower farmer, and it wasn't like she was in it for the money, anyway. We talked about how she should've built a sturdy plastic cage instead of trusting cheap wire fences because squirrels can chew through almost anything if they want to badly enough, and then she said something I didn't expect: "I'm worried about you. You haven't been home for over a year now. Where are you living? What's that noise?"

I wanted to say, "A lot of things happened, and it got hard to be around these people all the time... But I like them." That would have been dishonest. We talked some more about my job, though, and hers. She wanted to set an example for her children by showing that everyone had to work, even rich people like us who could afford not to. It's easy to imagine that parents would say stuff like that—but years later, it was still the truth.

I'd been hearing a noise, really more of a rumble, all along through the phone and was just then becoming aware that it wasn't an outside thing at all. I looked up from the grass of the lawn outside the gym to find Arnaud crossing the parking lot with paint brushes stuck in his pants.

You could smell it off him, that strange tallow scent of wet paint before the solvents irritate your upper respiratory passages—you know, like freshly peeled carrots. He tossed down his brushes and lit a cigarette. What was happening to me? Even though I didn't care about us being together anymore, this obviously wasn't something I wanted to see while talking to my mother. I saw my father calling back again, his eyes white slits between droopy lids, his arm stretched across the couch to pick up the phone. He wore headphones but didn't have them on. I could hear Arnaud crawling into bed with someone upstairs where it was dark, and then I heard her whisper sweetly about closing her eyes—a voice only babies and tape recorders can understand or simulate well.

I was consumed with bilious jealousy and irrepressible lust. A deep, burning shame climbed up my esophagus and into my cheeks. Warm blood flushed my loins. I looked down and saw that my arms were covered in goosebumps, stiff and crinkly like the skin of old people. All I could think about was fucking Arnaud, his voice when he came, how it sounded like an alien in a movie, and how hot it was, and how it shouldn't be. I wanted to grip his cock until it burst into pieces in my fist. My mother was telling me something I couldn't hear, but it didn't matter—she was crying and talking about how when we were younger we used to go crabbing together at Lake Michigan every weekend when Dad worked for Boeing full time and how when she retired they moved up to the Bluffs because she wanted to be closer to her family and it was pretty up there, but now that Dad's gone, the house is too large.

Just then, Arnaud turned around at the door and pulled down his crotch zipper, exposing himself so brazenly I was certain my mother could see every inch of him through my headset; he stepped out onto the balcony without underwear and began pissing over the rail. The headset slid out of my hand and clunked noisily to the ground; it was like a joke I'd missed somehow, but there was nobody around who would find such antics even remotely humorous.

I hung up on my mom and went back into the gym and did seventy chest presses, hoping to burn off the feeling. The image of Arnaud lingered in my mind. I did a few more above my normal maximum, but it didn't work, and I ended up masturbating in the shower while I watched people undress in the changing room. When I walked out, they looked at me like how an artist feels when the art doesn't come out right. I felt like the kind of person who sneaks up on others and takes pictures of them naked—someone with dirty, perverted intentions, a criminal. I felt like a statue burning in the desert, an inanimate object, unable to scream.

11.

Sweet Head Dragon, man, 2018

I decided to break it off with Arnaud. Despite his pretension, I always found myself overwhelmed by a sense of authority when I was with him. His voice would float over steaming black cod and drill into me, pushing me down, and I would submit. And so I could never say outright, "I think we should stop seeing each other." I had to find another way.

The next night that we went out, I talked to him more than I usually would, which of course he took as an opening. He said things like: "I've had such a good time with you so far," and, "I'm really starting to think there's more here than I initially imagined."

I nodded politely and smiled, ordering another beer. Feeling bad that we hadn't gotten along in the past—and encouraged by his unguarded behavior—I told him that I had been feeling homesick recently and that there wasn't as much for me to do in the city as there had been a couple weeks ago.

He tapped his fingers on the table and nodded vigorously with a scowl on his face, which looked absurdly feminine. After a few minutes, I could feel the warmth of tears starting to swell up behind my eyes and quickly excused myself to go pee. He followed me, grabbed my arm and turned it around so that he could look at my watch—I'd just bought that one yesterday, actually—and then kissed me behind the ear. I slipped away from him immediately. I couldn't help it—I felt a knot in my stomach and started to cry.

The waterworks came before the words did: just a flurry of expletives between tears that elicited little sympathy from him at first. But then, when he figured out it was an emotional outburst, he apologized piteously, took my hand, and asked to come upstairs. I'd hoped that following him would be like taking a pill to halt an anxiety attack, but it only seemed to make things worse. Upstairs, he tried to grind me against the wall. We fucked. He came like an alien. Then I started telling him I loved him. Over and over like a thunderstorm in the desert I told him I loved him, I was in love with him, until he grew cold and damp and seemed to wash away. The next morning he was gone, and I never heard from him again.

Needless to say, this precipitated a crash. I spent a week in my basement room hugging the plush toys I'd saved from when I was little and trying to quit smoking for real this time. Then another week in my room crying in abject heartbreak over Arnaud—torn between sobbing uncontrollably every hour on the hour or disappearing into a dry, brief coma, during which all I did was eat Cheetos and play Wolfenstein on the Internet.

Arnaud destroyed something elemental in me. He'd been my puppet, and I'd been his. I felt like a used toy, discarded with his trash. This lasted for two weeks, then three. It's funny how the world turns normally even when you're in free fall; people get laid off, get married, or are born into trouble wherever you go, and time goes on without interruption, maybe because it has no other choice.

The owners of the house would appear like mosquitoes out of nowhere, looking for blood. One of them was signing off on the environmental renovations, walking through the property, taking pictures, and making notes on a clipboard. When she came to my room, where the soft pulse of ocean tide beat like a subsonic drum, she checked the affect recognition system, running through a diagnostic series of pained facial expressions, apologizing for interrupting my obviously important work, and mentioned they were looking to fill a slot at a rave the next weekend.

I was eager for any distraction from my neurosis, and for a variety of reasons, I found myself excited to do more drugs. Specifically, I wanted something that would motivate me to clean the house. Plus, free stuff was always nice, so I volunteered on the spot. One of her two equally pale friends who helped run things began interjecting ambiguous asides about lighting and security. He was wearing what looked like distressed sweatpants with huge cargo pockets and a camo bandana. He kept swinging a set of keys on a yin-yang keychain in a loose rhythm that jerked me in and out of a trance. I found myself instinctively following his movements with my eyes. They told me I could make seven hundred dollars for a single night's work. I accepted the gig.

12.

The Bow crew likes bows, 2020

The night of the gig, my Uber was late. The night air grew colder as I grew more anxious. Finally, a car pulled up, and a man with a skullcap rolled down the window and waved me over. I got in. The driver claimed he'd been held up at a West Hollywood hotel where he'd waited on his previous fare, this eccentric elderly lady who'd tried to introduce herself as "Grace Underthrust." She'd commended him on the beauty of his shirt.

"Where are you taking me?" I said after forty-five minutes of silence. The part of town we were in looked forbidding, populated by warehouses and parking lots. "You don't have to answer that." I told myself, "They didn't force their way into your home for this gig, after all." But something about it gave me the creeps right away, so when he ignored my question and continued driving, I decided to get out.

"You can't tell me you haven't been here before," he said, slamming the car into park with a jolt that pried my arm from the seatbelt clasp. His words were razor-edged, and his face was composed with pinpoint precision. The driver started crawling around on his seat, trying to stop whatever it was banging against my door.

I saw that the roof of the car was covered in birdseed, which started spilling out over the side. He got angry when I didn't respond. He ranted about how he used to keep cardinals outside his house, but since they ate all his plants, they'd had to go. Then he started in on how the neighborhood had changed over the years and how the birds ate all his fish. He told me he'd recently named them after celebrities but lost track of it when they multiplied so fast. Then I realized with horror that there were hundreds of them, little blackbirds forming tight black circles with their wings.

They came in through my half-open window and stuck to my face like Velcro. I wrestled with the door handle, terrified. This had to be some sort of initiation ritual for their rave operation. After a moment that felt like eternity, I got out and walked toward the warehouse—then he started shouting at me from his car until his voice went hoarse and faint in the background.

The structure was completely anonymous from the outside. Only a subtle sign with silver lettering told me I was in the right place. The attitude of nocturnal youth culture felt absent. I walked up to the door and waited for an attendant dressed like a mall sweepstakes queen to show me inside. A young woman with pigtails was wheeling around an empty wheelchair. People laughed at this for reasons that were completely unfathomable to me. I tried to steer clear of the wheelchair, but on its second lap it caught my leg and spilled me onto the floor. Several people gathered and began filming me. Before they could do any serious damage, two white women in neoprene bodysuits rescued me and escorted me through an unmarked door. They led me down a long hallway. That empty spot was where the club proper began.

Still unsure of what was happening, I entered a vast mezzanine enclosed by columns. I could only see the ceiling; there were no other vantage points. The first people I saw started dancing. They moved like machines with awkward jerks to their heads and shoulders. Their bodies didn't distinguish between left and right. They watched each other closely, preying on any hint of deviation or indecision. I stood frozen at first. But after a few minutes, the music started pulling me down to the floor with an irresistible friction to my eardrums, and what followed was, as they say, a blur: a quick, steady succession of lights and colored liquids pulsing through my mouth and ears as I took in the atmosphere.

"There's a guy over there whose nostrils are bleeding," I heard one of my protectors yell into my ear. "You should talk to him. He'll take you to the DJ booth. Your set starts in ten minutes."

13.

The Seer, 2021

I took a moment to collect myself before introducing myself to everyone in the DJ booth. There were six or seven people there, all of whom I'd mistaken for the same few entities over and over. One guy had a purple piercing in his lower lip, which didn't seem very relevant to me—I was trying to find someone who looked like they understood music. When the girl with pigtails appeared out of nowhere and began asking if I wanted a shot from a tequila bottle, I asked if she had anything stronger. She produced a bag of powder from her fanny pack, which she upended into a five hundred-milliliter water bottle of vodka sitting on the console.

"Can I get more coke?" I asked her. "It's not really dissolving."

She shrugged.

When it was time for me to mix out of the previous DJ with the purple piercing, I cued up a vintage house banger and let it play for a few bars. The purple-pierced guy was texting someone about getting out of here, and the rest were straining their ears with faces that said they'd rather be anywhere but here. I worked hard to try and seem casual, like this was something I did every day at six in the morning. A few people began to bob their heads along with the beat: a guy in a baseball cap and another wearing a reflective vest. The one texting looked up from his phone and started going through these weird contortions with his hands that took several minutes for him to complete. I kind of got lost in the motions, and soon the track was finishing up, and I had nothing else cued. Silence sucked into the room like a smashed light bulb, then the voices of the thinning crowd began to take over, demanding an explanation.

"Everybody ready?" a voice interrupted from the ceiling and walls all around us. "Listen up: we're going into a sensory deprivation phase for the next sixty minutes. This music will be fed through your bodies so you won't know when anything starts or stops."

There was an anti-decibel device floating next to me that emanated a frigid, insectile buzzing sound. I had taken too much coke on an empty stomach; for the first time in years, I was trying not to throw up. I ran for the dressing room, burst through the door past a table covered with foil-wrapped pills, slammed into a wall that wasn't there, then stumbled out the other side to discover that I was lost in a maze of staircases and unmarked rooms. The music had stopped flowing from its source but kept going inside me. Time not only warped—it completely disappeared. I could see far-off light sources like dead stars in a primordial universe. It was the longest night of my life, but it felt like no time had passed at all when bloodred lights began to pulse and I found myself back where I started.

I heard myself speaking out loud.

"Fuck this," somebody said in a voice that sounded completely different than mine. "I'm not going to play. I just want to dance."

"I don't even think you're in the right room, sweetheart," a girl answered. "You better get back where you belong fast, or they'll come for you." Her voice crackled like a conference call from five countries away.

I was lying on the floor in the dressing room. Purple-pierced guy handed me a bottle of water to rinse out my mouth, along with some pills that looked like aspirin but were probably opiates. I remembered looking at his text conversation about getting the fuck out of here by any means necessary, and suddenly all attention turned toward me as though what I did would decide the fate of their entire group. The first pounding bass beat dropped, and purple-pierced guy took a sideways glance before lunging—like a wolf at a breakfast buffet—toward me, thrusting his head against my neck as the music got louder and louder. It was over in seconds.

14.

Tonight is the night, full monty, 2018

I walked back outside in a daze, trying not to think about what happened in there. Every part of my body was buzzing with a weird chemical high. It was dark enough to see the stars without being blinded by the sun coming up over Los Angeles, and I watched a group of youngish but seasoned-looking people march in a straight line through one corner of the street, instantly grabbing my attention.

They were dressed fairly uniformly. They wore skinny jeans and cheap boots that came halfway up their shins. There was something definitely otherworldly about them—about the way they moved, their facial expressions devoid of any human feeling.

I followed to get a closer look at these people. The group in front of me changed formation into a kind of tight knot with hands on each other's backs. They were reciting something to each other in low voices, half-muffled by the general din that had begun around them. Once or twice I heard the name "Tate Haus" mentioned—something about "Old Man Woodbine" being reborn. It was strange—the notion of old dudes traveling in packs through the night was not new to me, but I had never seen such a clearly defined group. As I walked closer and they started to disperse, their energy began to permeate my system, replacing the chemicals that had been running through it.

There was something totally unidentifiable about them—"a quaintly dysfunctional family," I remember thinking as I watched them fade into the crowd. Most of them were wearing dark purple robes with a large "T" emblazoned across their chests, and when I looked more closely at the letters, they began to ooze down onto my retina through my eyelids so that when I looked up again a few minutes later, the letter had completely disappeared.

Apparently, I was standing at the edge of a drainage canal. The surface sparkled under the violet glow of streetlamps, stirring up phantasmic visions in my mind's eye. There were three deep grooves, one on top of another—the bottom one filled with dead leaves and trash. Things always looked the same way whenever I experimented with drugs—maybe most things do, but it was easy enough for my imagination to populate them with strange figures standing in rows on either side of me.

It would have been easier for me then to simply let myself slip into one of those trenches and wash out this contamination. The longer I stayed, the colder I felt, like my veins were full of cold water instead of blood. But it wasn't me feeling this—it was something outside me, something that was slipping inside my skin without asking permission or offering instructions on what to do with itself once it got there. It moved through me like a liquid, finding places I hadn't noticed until it showed them to me. The world was no longer an innocent net of laws and blessings—one brimming with miraculous opportunities for the individual—but, instead, something closer every minute to being inside my body or entering into a relationship with it that would result in obsolescence. It wouldn't be long before the cold night air would freeze my body into a cocoon of ice, leaving only one open mouth for me to scream.

15.

Travelers of fortune, 2019

The next thing I remembered was someone grabbing my wrists behind me and pushing buttons on her phone to reveal her name: Carrie Sweetwater, Patient Advocate/Social Worker at The Fishbowl Consortium's Los Angeles Rehabilitation Facility. She was having trouble holding on to me as I struggled against her. Something was yanking on my shoulders as the stars rushed across the sky to meet us, and as we gained speed, they became brighter and more colorful; it would have been magnificent if I had been able to stop watching them long enough to really see anything else.

The next few days were spent surrounded by other people like myself: all of us there for the same reason, all of us looking for forms of calm to surround ourselves with. Some people simply stopped—stopped talking and eating and moved so far inside their own minds that you could see them marching around in there like soldiers. Others were too loud, or ventured beyond the edges of common sense so far that it seemed almost natural when they got locked up again the next week, just the same way that the sea swallows up chunks of earth—the only constant truth in this world being that everything falls apart eventually, so why not you?

The rest of us fell somewhere in between. These people were painted with bright colors, patterns I never realized existed. The Fishbowl was an old rehab facility in East Los Angeles where they took abandoned structures and made them into their own—there was a ping-pong room that doubled as a functional cafe but also housed some of the coolest art I'd ever seen. The staff had just started working at the Fishbowl recently, and they seemed to care more about getting us healthy than keeping things up to code, so we took advantage of it whenever we could. There were any number of painters and comedians coming through the Fishbowl with me, some of whom I knew before they ended up in rehab, some who I met later.

There were three guitarists in there—the older one named Alkaline Burns was Black but sang like a white man; he played hard rock that would make you nod your head more than anything else. The next one down had red hair and a wildly energetic beard; his face was always an open window into how lonely he felt, even though I'm pretty sure most people took pity on him. And the youngest one was a bit of a Juggalo-wannabe named Theodora Nordok. He didn't talk much or open up to people unless they asked him a question.

Most of our days consisted of activities geared toward getting us all healthy again, but none more than our workshops with a woman named Sita Swamy who had been a performer in her youth and now ran a New Age workshop at the facility. What we did mostly was dance—the kind of dancing you do when no one is watching, no style of music playing but your own heartbeat. We found ways to shake off our spiritual curses by breaking them down into their constituent elements until there was nothing but us standing in the middle of it all, shaking off "just what the fuck" we were going to do from there.

We ate brown rice and smoothies and baked dairy-free chocolate chip cookies and rode stationary bikes on the second floor balcony of the building as traffic clogged up below us. But more than all those things, we danced freely—not as a statement about how things should be in this cold world, but just simply because your feet want to move when your heart wants to open.

We sang out through our pain, laughs ringing back in return—living in a world where all forms are temporary, but compassion for one another never ends. The sheer volume that the human voice is capable of seemed utterly inexhaustible then, pushing past barriers that exist solely in our minds rather than in blood and bone—toward some transcendental whole unto itself that we can't even begin to imagine until we need it and hope beyond all else that it will find us.

One of the staffers at the Fishbowl gave me a hardcover copy of *The Book* by somebody named Franklin Jones. He was great at working with alcoholics and addicts because there weren't any rules or guidelines to getting better, except for what you needed. Much of our time at the Fishbowl was spent talking to one another and trying on new ideas—but maybe not as much as it should have been. Most people didn't even finish reading the first chapter of his book, but he stressed that it had nothing to do with their ability to heal or whether they were ready for the world outside those walls; what's more important is that you're open to finding new things beyond your understanding of the way the world works.

There's a page in there where Franklin Jones asks us to take an empty box and put ourselves inside it, telling us that it doesn't matter what we place inside the box because the point of this exercise is not about creating a stable environment for ourselves, but making one long enough for us to demonstrate our ability to endure it. He says that once we've done this, we can take our box and start filling it up with other boxes, until the empty space inside us becomes small enough for us to fit through. Then he gives instructions on how to navigate around all of these boxed lives until the world starts looking like you want it to—or, at least, different than you thought was possible before you started slowing down in the corners of your mind in order to see what was in front of you.

I didn't bring *The Book* with me when I snuck out of the Fishbowl. You can't always take everything with you. I left my roommate a letter shoved underneath her bed before everyone woke up—just the essentials of my soul scribbled out, breathing through my fingers and filling up the page until I couldn't make any more empty space to write with.

16.

Triff mich beim Baum (Meet me by the Tree), 2018

My room at the TikTok house had been filled with concrete. The water was rising and the foundation of the house had begun to decay. I rented a place in Venice. I could walk to the beach in ten minutes and pick up a vegan croissant on the way from a little cafe that looked like it had been decorated by 1980s hippies then sealed in amber. I was reading books again. I'd already finished *The Book*, and I started in on another one by a writer named Joseph Campbell. I don't remember now what he said about whatever it is you're supposed to find when you follow your bliss.

I did find out just how hard it is to find anything when you think you already know where it's hidden, that somewhere in your hands are the keys to unlock its secret—but everything around you makes it hard to locate, especially with all of what comes out through your mouth when you talk about the random things life throws in front of you. I started going over my writing again.

My notebook was filling up quickly. There was a whole world inside of me, living words I'd never really paid attention to—my thoughts released into the open air. And it doesn't matter what you think you know or who you are because once there's paper in front of your eyes and something burning through your blood too hot for even the sky to hold, there isn't any holding back whatever is left.

I started attending a Catholic Church. The architecture was all wrong. The arches were all different sizes, and the steeple wasn't tall enough. The congregation dressed badly, in blue jeans and plain dresses. The priest looked like a businessman, not a man ready to lead people to salvation. But they listened silently when he talked for over an hour about how all were welcome unto God—that there was nothing so bad that He couldn't fix if one only believed in Him strongly enough. That meant accepting one's true self, forgiving others of their sins, and often failing to become perfect individuals.

I found, while staring into my notebook, that I no longer believed. That line in *The Book* where Franklin Jones says that you have to tolerate any life for long enough for your eyes to adjust. To sit through all of this world's bullshit without wanting to give up or break down because it's too much, or having seen something so beautiful you can't explain how it made you feel about what came before it. To have patience in the world when nothing seems to make any sense at all, and why should it because we don't even know what "making sense" means? Making sense didn't make sense, and I couldn't make any sense of it all, least of all the church.

I decided to try another church. The second one was in Los Feliz. It was Christian, but it was never clear to me what the precise denomination was. There was valet parking, and most of the cars were Audis and Teslas; sometimes there were Subarus. The pastor wore a Patagonia fleece when he preached from what resembled a stage more than a pulpit. He showed slides of his family vacation with his beautiful wife and blond children. He talked about how we needed to be more like God and less like men, especially since we had this disease called "egocentrism" that made us scared of anything beyond ourselves. He said it was okay to hope for better lives and that we were allowed in higher places than the life we already led.

Sometimes they played Christian rock music (sometimes Christian rap) instead of gospel songs or hymns. The sermons were long, and the kids in the back would start to fall asleep, their heads resting on each other's shoulders or their mouths hanging open out of boredom. They always seemed so alone, so far away from everything.

The church was secluded behind tall hedges that shielded it from the street. It was surrounded by groves of trees with thick, stinking cobwebs hanging down and white flowers sprouting up through the brown mulch beneath them. I felt like this place had stood forever even though it was no older than Hollywood itself, that if you looked back far enough into history you'd find yourself gazing upon our era's replica of events that happened long ago.

I walked out one Sunday, midway through the service. It was a sunny day, and I decided not to take a bus or call an Uber, just to walk through the strip malls and crosswalks and encampments until I arrived back at the TikTok house again—the place where everything started and should've ended because no one really belonged there, or at least I didn't.

There were a lot of things driving me back to the TikTok house again—something about a band I saw playing in a nightclub on Sunset Boulevard with a singer who looked like he was born sometime during World War II, wearing an old field jacket from Korea. The lead singer had such a thin, frail voice, you could swear he'd be eaten alive by the noise. My heart cracked open when I heard him sing, and I smiled with perfect joy when Maria took my hand that night and we found someplace quiet where we could talk, where everything fell into silence, and she told me she had seen God, that I could see God, too. And then there was this city that held so much hope—the hopes of people who believed that one day there would be an answer to all our questions, that love was the only thing that mattered in this world—and maybe it is. Maybe life's just one big house party with no working toilets and little to drink, but everybody's full of hope because they believe in something so strong, so pure—something greater than themselves.

I hadn't found out yet, though, what exactly that was, but every day it seemed a little closer to me. The freedom from our pasts, the freedom of living in a time when we have everything from one hundred cable TV channels and six hundred live music clubs to life being so short you have no choice but to do what you want or lose your mind inside all these things—the fast movement of time and passing of the seasons, years flying past without many things changing, except a few parts that you want to be able to show to your grandchildren as proof that everything is okay, even when it doesn't look like it.

17.

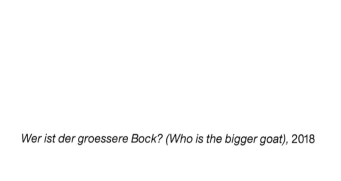

Wer ist der groessere Bock? (Who is the bigger goat), 2018

When I got to the TikTok house, I didn't recognize anyone. Jaden, Jordice, Briden, Rheagar, none of them were there. There was only an English-accent guy (he had an Australia baseball cap on) and a Victorian-looking girl with huge breasts that seemed unreal, like they were the second breast implants anyone ever got. They asked me if I had a band. "No," I said, looking around the room for whomever else I used to know—how long was everyone gone? Where did they go? Did they all die together in some fucked-up accident inside their self-made world? Was this place cursed because it never let anyone be happy here for more than a couple weeks? Or maybe what they said was true—that all things really do happen for a reason, and it's up to us to figure out what those reasons were, and only then will we know how anything fits together.

The English-accent guy gave me directions to where I could find food or whatever on the beach, even though I didn't need them and hadn't asked. "Did you know there's this great Indian restaurant on the boardwalk? It's named Aaj India, but they call it The Joint—and their samosas are incredible. They're this crispy pastry stuffed with potatoes and some kind of meat that tastes better than it sounds. You can't go wrong if you get them for an app or dinner. They serve beer, too," he said. I ended up eating there, and the food was as good as he said it would be.

I decided that the disappearance of the TikTok boys was a gift from the universe, maybe even from the multiverse, a sign that I had switched tracks, that I'd leapt onto another timeline or into a better world where I was free to believe in anything I chose to. To believe in dying hard on some distant day, written out of creation with our names etched on tombstones covered with branches or flowers—everything else put through the trash compactor. Some people don't see it that way, but I think everything is meant to be beautiful if you live long enough to recognize its beauty.

18.

Who are we riding?, 2018

The woods are always waiting behind the trees beyond Hollywood Boulevard, about two streets before you hit Franklin Avenue. You just need to know where to find them—where the streets that lead into darkness start, all alone and away from everything; even when it's broad daylight in the city, no one seems to believe in what might be hiding back there. And when I found them, I fell down like a drunk who passed out after drinking too many tall boys—a place where the air fills your lungs and makes you feel like someone's there with you, even while they're not. The woods were always waiting— we didn't make them, we don't own them, but our presence in time can witness what they want us to; maybe it's an explanation for all the shit that comes along with dreaming about doing something greater than ourselves—something better in a world where we're all perfect mistakes.

The woods replaced the church for a while. I could always find the entrance—between those two old walls covered in graffiti—from those concrete stairs that led up the hill just beside the school where children drilled mathematics into their brains as I walked by.

There used to be a sign that said, "Private Property—Go Away Or We Will Tell!" When I looked closely, I could still see its faded letters hidden behind layers of paint. When night fell in frustration, the heat absorbing through all of our bodies until all that's left is sweat drinking down each one of us, behind those trails of trees that a million cars have passed every day, pushing past branches and leaves in one continuous flow of power, I followed one line at a time until I found myself there, standing next to the sign that said, "PRIVATE PROPERTY," my feet temporarily frozen in place, staring across fifty feet of distance with nothing but dry leaves scraping against each other like lips smacking wine glasses.

I never saw anything strange there.

19.

Zaumgschwoasst (Soldered), 2018

I did return to the church. The truth was that I missed the pastor and his slightly receding hair and performance outerwear. I missed eavesdropping on the churchgoers. I missed the Sheetrock walls and the valet station umbrella. One day I walked in late. There were no seats open in the back with the sleeping kids. I was forced to walk the arcade up to the front-most pew. As the service inched along, I couldn't take my eyes off of him up there. He had this way about him that was different from the last time I'd seen him. Then, he seemed to always teeter on foreboding cliff faces while trying not to fall into deep waters below, because what happened in church would also happen inside our own minds. This man looked better than before, though—healthy and happy. Maybe he had found that place where all things started and would end, or maybe God was too busy to deal with him anymore because the afterlife happens only in the finite light of our own imaginations, not inside any physical realm we can find. As he spoke on and on about sin and redemption of our souls, I stared at him. Maybe it was something personal between us, or maybe we shared some kind of bond—maybe even a karmic connection—where neither one of us could really go wrong if we reached out to each other in the dark with an open heart because, for once, there would be no fear.

Suddenly, in the middle of a prayer, his eyes opened up as if he saw me on the other end of an imaginary line and he stopped—just like that. He stared right at me, then continued the prayer with eyes open, hoping I'd listen to him, though I could hardly hear him over the rush of blood in my ears.

"In order to be saved, there are three things you must have: your sin, knowledge of your sin, and a Savior. In order to know this, there is only one way: the Church. The Church will show you that you are sinners in order to be washed from those sins by accepting Jesus as your Savior—the only choice that can save us all. Pray with me now if you believe or if you feel something special, like the spirit of a loved one come here to speak to your soul."

He raised his hands up in the air and fed off those prayers as if he were drowning in an ocean with no landmass anywhere, thirsty for precious water. Specks of sweat sent ripples through my vision like tiny undersea creatures swimming down from above.

After the sermon, I approached him, queuing up in a line of mild, adoring worshipers. He greeted me with an outstretched hand that was hot and moist to the touch. I felt like he could sense something about me there underneath my skin, like an electric current sparking through my flesh down into his palm. He smiled at me as if he'd seen me walking up to him in a dream. I gave him my name, and he didn't flinch, even though there was something eager in his eyes. Within a week, we were sleeping together.

The service was always moving. It all felt like a sex ritual—a final purging of the soul as it left the body. He quoted the Bible like an erotic poem. When we made love, I didn't climax, except when I thought of his wife and her depleted libido, victim of a pharmaceutical pill. When I did, I cried, and this seemed to give him some deep satisfaction or sense of accomplishment or power. Instead of orgasms, I experienced the cleanest emptiness, as if I were being scoured by a scalding spotlight. The crown of my head would crack open and golden honey would gush out of it, down my skull and into my limbs to the tips of my fingers and toes. Its sweetness was knowledge beyond good and evil. It was the resurrection of my life. For this I thanked him silently.

20.

Zweikoepfig (Double Headed), 2018

I never shared anything of my personal life with him. When we were together, I was purified nothingness. He erased my past, my present, my memories. This process went on for months, maybe even years—time became very blurry during that intense period. One day he asked me to go with him to the church glamping retreat at some beachfront property where people could come and pray all day or just relax and not be bothered by anyone else that they didn't already know through the church; everyone was close enough that they could trust each other. I agreed. The place wasn't beachfront, but it was still pretty nice. There was the sound of waves lapping against the shore, and you could hear the whisper of wind through pines. The ground was perfectly soft—like marshmallow fluff. Inside every tent were mattresses, blankets, pillows—all provided by other members that I'd never met before or didn't recognize in passing moments because it's hard to look directly at anyone's face when you're trying desperately to conceal a secret. There were about ten or twelve of us total there, including the pastor and his wife, both of them looking very happy together. I wondered if they ever fucked anymore. Maybe they just held each other all night in a bizarre, sexless waiting game that would take a lifetime to complete.

When everyone else had left for their day, we walked up two separate trails into the pines and met and touched each other and found ourselves as empty as the sky on a dark winter night. We'd freed ourselves from a magic spell, giving back life to fleshy limbs, only so that they could tug us apart again. There wasn't any orgasm for me at all again because this was an act of worship and purification. Then came the void, then that moment when we remembered who we were, what we were doing, and that no one else could ever know, and I imagined him in the tent and I saw it collapsing, crushing him under the weight of hubris. As we walked down the mountain, something told me our time was almost over. I offered a little of myself, a hook on which I'd hung some hope.

"My friend Maria says a tribe from Brazil is coming to Malibu. To do a ritual. She says you can see God." He said nothing, only trudging toward the place where the trail forked. "She says they can show you. She says she saw God."

All that mattered was the pleasure between us.

What happened next, I remember two ways. I heard him say it in a sermon there on the beach, in front of the white, bell-shaped glamping tents and the group of worshipers, his rage-filled voice trapped in his throat like a wild boar in a tiny pit. I also remember him tossing beside me in a dark bed, his voice slurred with sleep, his hair damp with sweat. I can see him turning to face me, his eyes glowing faintly red. His words are etched like scripture in my mind, like infected scars on my calves:

"This is a war with the savage. It has gone on for hundreds of years. The forces of darkness and ignorance seek to deceive us. The primal forces of the occult. All the rotting bones and hair, puked up from the bowels to deceive us. They are animals, possessed by demons. We must drive them off the face of the Earth. We must show them no mercy. The devil is in their blood."

This is the last I remember of him. I stopped attending services. His pictures disappeared from my phone. In one of those pictures, I could see his wife praying over him with a worried look on her face, as if he were fighting some kind of dragon inside his own head. Or maybe he was no longer willing to play God and had become cryptic about it all because who really believed in what he was selling, anyway? I was ashamed to have found a part of my soul in him. I felt as if I'd joined a cult, left my church forever, and gone down the same road as all those others. Even now, that is all I remember—a serpent eating its own tail into peace through pain-wracked screams so loud they echo through the starry sky.

DRAWINGS COURTESY OF LYDIA MARIA PFEFFER AND OCHI

ACKNOWLEDGEMENTS

The author would like to thank:

Lydia Maria Pfeffer for her drawings.

Violet Office for their cover art.

Emily Segal for prompting this book.

And all of Deluge Books for their guidance and support.

Amor Cringe was written using OpenAI's generative AI language model, GPT-3.

BIO

K Allado-McDowell is a writer, speaker, and musician. They are the author, with GPT-3, of the books *Pharmako-AI* and *Amor Cringe*, and are co-editor of *The Atlas of Anomalous AI*. They record and release music under the name Qenric.

Allado-McDowell established the Artists + Machine Intelligence program at Google AI. They are a conference speaker, educator and consultant to think-tanks and institutions seeking to align their work with deeper traditions of human understanding.

Also From Deluge Books

Mercury Retrograde
A Novel by Emily Segal

Black Venus Fly Trap
Poems by Jeanetta Rich

Tricking Hour
Essays by Irene Silt

My Pleasure
Poems by Irene Silt

delugebooks.com

CPSIA information can be obtained
at www.ICGtesting.com
Printed in the USA
LVHW081521070722
722893LV00012B/231

9 781736 210437